Located in a strange, parallel the once-peace is in danger from a the ferocious Volca Magmion, they will stop at nothing to take over the island and capture the Gormiti from the peaceful nations of Gorm – Sea, Air, Earth and Forest.

Nick, Toby, Lucas and Jessica – four ordinary schoolkids – are Gorm's only hope. Recruited by Razzle, their talking lizard guide, they head to Gorm whenever trouble calls. Because if they don't stop Magmion and the Volcano Gormiti from conquering Gorm, its cosmic connection to Earth will cause both worlds to fall!

LET'S GO!

MEET THE CHARACTERS

Nick, the Lord of Earth
Brainy and a bit of a know-it-all

Toby, the Lord of Sea
He loves pulling pranks on his friends

Lucas, the Lord of Forest
Easy-going, he always roots for the underdog

Jessica, the Lord of Air
Her favourite hobbies are judo and shopping

Razzle

A talking lizard who knows all about Gorm

Gina

She's Jessica's best friend, and has a crush on Lucas

Magmion, the Lord of Magma

His evil aim is to take over all of Gorm

Troncalion

The Ancient Guardian of Forest

Drakkon

The Ancient Guardian of Volcano

Tentaclion
The Ancient Guardian of Sea

Roscalion
The Ancient Guardian of Earth

Ike Pinkney
The biggest bully at Venture Falls
Junior High School

Mr and Mrs Tripp
Nick and Toby's parents

Firespitter
A Volcano Gormiti with
a hypnotising eye

Delos

A Sea Gormiti with
a tentacle arm

Mantra

An intelligent and wise
Sea Gormiti

Crabs the Avenger

A powerful Sea Gormiti with
claw hands

Helico the Wary

A Sea Gormiti with deadly
drills for arms

EGMONT

We bring stories to life

First published in Great Britain 2011
by Egmont UK Limited
239 Kensington High Street
London W8 6SA

Gormiti Series and Images from the Series: © 2011
Giochi Preziosi S.p.A and Marathon and all related logos,
names and distinctive likenesses are the exclusive
property of GIOCHI PREZIOSI and MARATHON.
Inspired by Leandro Consumi's original work "Gormiti"
Text © 2011 Egmont UK Limited
All rights reserved.

Adapted by Barry Hutchison

ISBN 978 1 4052 5683 4
1 3 5 7 9 10 8 6 4 2
Printed and bound in Great Britain by the CPI Group

FSC
Mixed Sources
Product group from well-managed
forests and other controlled sources

Cert no. TT-COC-002332
www.fsc.org
© 1996 Forest Stewardship Council

Egmont is passionate about helping to preserve the world's remaining ancient forests.
We only use paper from legal and sustainable forest sources.

This book is made from paper certified by the Forestry Stewardship Council (FSC),
an organisation dedicated to promoting responsible management of forest resources.
For more information on the FSC, please visit www.fsc.org. To learn more about
Egmont's sustainable paper policy, please visit www.egmont.co.uk/ethical

Beastly
and
Keeper Kept

CAN'T GET ENOUGH GORMITI ACTION?

Now available:

The Fog and Going Green

Coming in June 2011:

The Lords of Fate and Shock to the System

The Root of Evil and Black Salt Diamonds

CONTENTS

CHAPTER ONE

A DOG'S LIFE

The full moon hung low in the sky above the Venture Falls Zoo, where most of the animals were asleep in their cages. The elephants lay snuggled together in their enclosure, their trunks wrapped around each other. The monkeys nestled in the branches of their tree, snoring softly. Even the lion, who usually slept with one eye open, was lost in peaceful dreams.

Suddenly, the night was split by a strange, supernatural howl. It seemed to come from nowhere, echoing across the darkened sky and startling the zoo animals awake.

Something about the sound panicked the animals. It was like nothing they'd ever heard before.

The elephants trumpeted wildly and stamped their feet. The monkeys leapt down from the trees, screeching and hollering as they tried to force their way through the narrow bars of their cage.

With a deafening roar, the lion hurled himself against the side of his enclosure, tearing at the wire mesh with his claws. The metal links were too strong for him to tear through, though, no matter how hard he tried.

And then, with a crash, a huge section of the enclosure collapsed, as the elephants thundered their way through the wall, battering away the bricks with the top of their heads. The collapsing wall took down part of the lion's fence.

Soon, with the howl still echoing through the night, almost every one of the zoo's animals was free and running as fast as they could away from that terrible sound.

The next morning, all was calm. The sun shone brightly down on Jessica and the two dogs she was walking near her house. The dogs woofed excitedly as Jessica scratched them both behind the ears.

'How goes our dog-walking biz, Jess?' asked Nick as he approached with his brother, Toby.

'You're looking at two satisfied customers,' Jessica beamed. 'You put up my flyers, right?'

'Natch,' nodded Toby, pointing to a telephone pole, where an advertising flyer for the dog-walking business had been pinned. 'And with the money we earn, we can afford the advance release of Skull Blasters 8000!'

Jessica shook her head and crossed her arms. 'Because what I need in my life are *more* video-game explosions,' she snorted, before opening her arms wide and prancing along the street like a catwalk model.

'No,' she trilled. 'Some of us need a new outfit for the Spring Fling party. I've already got an outfit for early spring and another for late spring ...' She caught the look of confusion on the boys' faces. 'Hello? This dance is a *mid*-spring thing,' she said, rolling her eyes. 'Pfft. Boys!'

Toby and Nick looked at each other. They would

never understand girls as long as they lived.

Jessica's mobile phone rung in her pocket. She pulled it out and her eyes lit up when she recognised the name on the caller ID.

'Gina!' she said, flipping open the phone. Gina was in all the same classes as Jessica, and the two had been best friends longer than either of them could remember. 'What's the word?'

'Already getting lots of calls on the flyers,' replied Gina. 'More dogs need walking – I'll text you the addresses.'

Jessica flipped the phone closed and did a twirl of excitement. 'Spring Fling, here we come!'

Just then, the sound of bounding footsteps made the children turn. Lucas ran up to them. He was out of breath, as much from excitement as from the half-mile he'd just run.

'Have you been watching the news?' he panted.

Toby shrugged. 'Only to see the sports bloopers. That stuff's awesome!'

'No, man, the Venture Falls Zoo? Last night?' Lucas looked around his friends, but none of them seemed to know what he was talking about. 'The animals totally busted out!'

'No way!'

'They caught all the animals except for one. A lion is still on the loose. It could be anywhere!'

Suddenly, one of the dogs down by Jessica's feet gave a low growl. The other quickly joined in, and the children soon realised what the animals were growling at. A large hedge beside them was rustling. Something was moving inside it.

'D-did you say a *lion*?' stammered Jessica, stepping back.

The green head of a small lizard poked up from inside the bush. Its reptile eyes were wide with panic. 'Lion?' he spluttered. 'Where?'

Razzle's sudden appearance surprised the children. They all leapt backwards, screaming with fright, before recognising their friend.

'Razzle!' said Jessica, sighing with annoyance and relief.

The dogs strained at their leads, jumping to try to get at the little lizard. Razzle darted up onto Nick's shoulder and perched there, out of reach of the dogs' teeth.

The chimes of Jessica's phone rang again. 'Hang on,' she said, before flipping it open. 'More calls about the flyer?'

'Business is booming,' laughed Gina. 'I'm going to need your help. I'm running out of hands!'

Jessica glanced over at Razzle. The lizard shook his head. 'Sorry, I'll help when I can,' said Jessica. 'But, um, something's come up ...'

'There are rumours in Gorm that Magmion has acquired a new steed – Drakkon!' said Razzle, gravely. He and the children were in the Primal Pad, looking through the Gorm Gate at the land of Gorm itself.

They watched as an enormous red and black

dragon emerged from inside a mountain and began swooping and diving through the sky.

'Drakkon is a Volcano Gormiti of great magical power,' Razzle continued. 'He's one of the Ancient Guardians.'

'Ancient Guardians?' frowned Nick. 'You're talking about immortal creatures than haven't been seen for, like, *ever*. I thought they were only legends.'

Beside him, Toby shook his head. 'Dude, seriously. How do you know all this stuff?'

Nick nodded in the direction of the Primal Pad library and adjusted his glasses. 'You like to watch sports bloopers. I like to read books on Gorm.'

Jessica was worried. 'So, if Drakkon really exists, and he's been found by Magmion ...'

'Sounds like a bad combo,' said Lucas.

'The worst,' confirmed Razzle. 'Your mission is to get to Gorm and to the bottom of these rumours.'

There was no time to lose. The children took up their positions by their power orbs.

'Elementals,' they cried together.

'Air!' said Jessica.

'Water!' said Toby.

'Forest!' added Lucas.

'Earth!' finished Nick.

'Reveal to us the Keeper, and give to them your chair,' they finished.

In the middle of the room, the Keeper's chair began to spin. Faster and faster it turned, the elemental emblems flickering across its back, one by one.

Razzle stepped closer as the chair began to slow. 'And the Keeper is ...'

With one final spin, the chair came to a stop and an icon lit up on its back.

'Air!' announced Razzle, just as the two dogs Jessica had been walking leapt up onto the seat and dozed off. Jessica cooed at their cuteness, and Razzle glared up at her. 'Could you keep your furry friends off the furniture?'

Jessica stepped past him, exchanging a high-five with Lucas as she made for the chair. 'Prepare to get your Gorm on, boys,' she smiled.

Shooing the dogs down from the chair, Jessica took their place. The chair rose into the air, bringing her level with the centre's control crystals.

'If Magmion's in the forest, then so are we,' Jessica said, moving the magic crystals around just

by waving her hands over them. All around the
Primal Pad, the other elemental crystals began to
glow.

A ripple passed across the surface of the Gorm Gate,
and the others knew it was time. Stepping up onto
the stone ledge which surrounded the circular hole
in the floor, Lucas, Nick, Toby and Razzle hopped
through the portal ... and vanished!

CHAPTER TWO

FACING THE GUARDIAN

The wind whipped at their faces and nipped their eyes as they plunged through the clouds, rocketing head-first towards the distant ground. The land of Gorm lay spread out below them. From here they could see each region, from the volcano to the sea. It was a spectacular sight, but one they didn't have much time to look at.

Back in the Primal Pad, Jessica watched her friends slow, then finally land. 'And – touchdown,' she said, with a smile. She flipped open a thick, leather-bound book and consulted its pages. 'OK, guys, Travel Tome says you're right on target.'

'No sign of Magmion,' replied Nick. He was leading the others through a twisting forest. Trees towered on either side of them, stretching far up above their heads.

'Are you sure?' asked Jessica. An image of her face appeared in a glowing sphere in front of the group. 'I'm picking up a major magic reading in your area.'

'Like, how major?' asked Nick.

'Like, *major* major.'

Lucas felt the hair on his arms stand on end. Jessica was right, there was definitely something going on. 'I'm sensing it, too,' he said. 'I feel all tingly.'

A rustling behind them made the boys turn. Up in the trees, some hanging vines and wide branches began to detach themselves from the treetops around them.

'It's the forest!' Lucas cried. 'It's alive!'

Nick shook his head. 'It's not the forest,' he said. 'It's *that.*'

A hulking creature pulled itself up to its full height and stepped over the trees. The beast was bigger than any the children had seen before, and seemed to be made from the very forest itself.

Leaves and branches grew from its thick, bark-like skin. Its legs were as thick as tree-trunks, and when its feet touched down, plants and vines grew in its steps.

The giant's shadow passed over the group. All Lucas could manage to say was, 'Whoa!'

Even Razzle seemed to be in awe. 'Ancient Guardian ...' he whispered.

'Drakkon?' asked Toby, his eyes still locked on the creature.

'No, this one's a Forest Ancient,' Razzle explained.

'That means it's true,' the little lizard realised. 'The Ancient Guardians of legend are returning to Gorm!'

Lucas took a few paces towards the beast, his hands outstretched.

'Dude, no sudden movements,' hissed Toby.

Ignoring him, Lucas walked closer to the giant creature. It looked down at him, but otherwise didn't react. 'It's OK,' Lucas assured the others. He knew he was in no danger from the Guardian. He could sense it. 'It's like we share an unspoken connection.'

'Makes sense,' nodded Razzle, stroking his chin. 'You're a Forest Gormiti, and so is this guy.'

Toby and Nick watched on in amazement as the creature slowly lowered its enormous head. Reaching up, Lucas gently stroked its rough skin, just as Jessica had done with the dogs.

As Lucas's hand touched the Ancient Guardian's hide, an electrical tingle passed through his entire body.

'Troncalion,' said Lucas, somehow picking up the creature's thoughts. 'His ... his name is Troncalion.'

Lucas's face suddenly went pale. 'And ... and he's *angry!*'

The mighty Guardian reared up onto his hind legs and let out a bellowing roar. His massive front legs came crashing down towards the ground – with Lucas still standing directly below.

Hurling himself at his friend, Toby slammed into Lucas with a flying rugby tackle. The two boys rolled to safety, just as Troncalion's feet hit the ground with a thunderous boom.

Troncalion lowered his head and charged towards the edge of the clearing. Each footstep shook the forest floor, like a series of small earthquakes.

Before the Ancient Guardian reached the trees, a flickering pyramid of energy appeared around him, forcing him to stop. He stood there, unmoving, his enormous frame held tightly in place.

'He's trapped,' gasped Lucas.

'Lock rocks,' explained Razzle. 'But I've never seen 'em this powerful before.'

A flicker of confusion passed across Nick's face. 'Lock rocks?'

Toby smirked. 'Hey, finally something you *don't* know.'

Before Nick could reply, a wide shadow swooped over them, cast by something large soaring high above them.

'What was that?' Toby asked nervously.

'I don't know,' Nick replied. Whatever it was, he didn't like it. 'Let's get this over with. Jessica?'

Back in the Primal Pad, Jessica flicked through the

pages of the enormous Travel Tome. 'Lock rocks, got it!' she announced. 'You're looking for three strategically placed magic crystals.'

The boys looked down at the forest floor around the trapped beast. Just a few metres in front of him, a glowing crystal poked up from the moss. They found two others behind and to the left of Troncalion, forming a triangle around him. The trio cautiously approached the closest crystal.

'The crystal triangulation must create some kind of magic snare,' Nick said.

Lucas shrugged. If the crystals were the problem, he had the perfect solution. Swinging back his leg, he prepared to kick them out of the way. Only a panicked screech from Razzle stopped him.

'Yikes!' the lizard yelped. 'D'you have any idea how much power is in those things? You've got to be very careful.'

'Razzle's right,' agreed Jessica. 'You want to bring all three of the crystals together over Troncalion,' she instructed, scanning the page. 'Carefully!'

Slowly, Lucas, Toby and Nick each bent down and picked up a crystal. The lock rocks glowed with raw magical energy in the boys' hands. All three boys walked towards Troncalion, holding the crystals above their heads.

But they soon encountered a problem. The Ancient Guardian was far too big for them to bring the crystals together above his head. Even at full stretch, their arms barely made it halfway up his giant legs.

'We can't reach,' moaned Nick.

Lucas concentrated, focusing on the psychic link he and Troncalion had shared. He had to make the Guardian realise they were trying to help him and that he had nothing to fear. Over and over, he willed him to understand.

Finally, with a low moan, Troncalion lowered to his knees and crouched down. He was still too tall for the boys to reach over, but now he was crouching they could at least climb up onto his back.

'Come on, it's cool,' urged Lucas, leading the way.

Clambering carefully, with only one hand to guide

them, the boys managed to drag themselves up onto Troncalion's wide shoulders. As soon as the crystals touched, the magical energy faded and the Ancient Guardian was free.

'Dude,' grinned Toby, impressed.

There was no time to celebrate, though. The large shadow swooped over them again and they felt Troncalion go tense. With a twitch of his powerful legs, the Guardian leapt forwards, forcing the boys to grab onto his vine-like hair to stop themselves falling off.

Suddenly, the spot where Troncalion had stood exploded in a searing-hot ball of flame. Everyone looked up to see an enormous, winged creature bearing down on them.

'Drakkon!' gasped Razzle.

The monstrous dragon opened its jaws, revealing a mouth full of sharp teeth and fire. And there, sitting astride the creature's back, was an equally terrifying figure.

Magmion!

CHAPTER THREE

BRAINWASHED

Drakkon let fly with another blast of fire, forcing Troncalion to lurch sideways. Lucas, Toby and Nick cried out as they were thrown from his shoulders. With a series of grunts, they landed hard on the forest floor.

Up on Drakkon's back, Magmion hissed with laughter. The evil Volcano Gormiti's snake-like eyes blazed with excitement as he glared down at Troncalion. 'You can meddle with my traps,' he bellowed, 'but you can't stop me from taming that beast.'

Leaping to his feet, Lucas cried, 'We'll see about that!'

Back in the Primal Pad, Jessica activated the elemental orbs. 'I'm on it, guys,' she announced. 'You're good to glow!'

The boys stood together, back to back, their eyes trained on the circling Drakkon. 'Elemental powers flow,' they chanted, as a swirl of energy flowed around them. 'Gormiti, Lords of Nature, go!'

As the magic began to alter the boys, Toby leapt into the air. His short, blond hair grew thicker and longer, transforming into strong tentacles. His skin grew tight around his bulging muscles, changing to a cool aqua blue.

'Power of the sea!' he cried.

Beside him, his brother was also changing. Nick was the smallest of the group, but he soon outgrew his friends as his body transformed into the living rock of his Earth Gormiti form.

'Strength of the stone!' he bellowed.

Lucas, too, had changed. In his place stood a hulking green figure whose body seemed to be made from the plants and trees themselves.

'Force of the forest!' he boomed, taking up his place next to his friends.

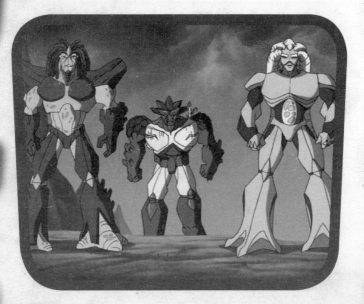

High in the sky, Magmion dug his knees into Drakkon's sides, bringing the flying Ancient Guardian swooping down towards the three heroes. 'Attack!' he commanded.

Opening his mouth wide, Drakkon sent a ball of fire scorching through the air towards the boys. Before it could find its target, though, the fireball was blocked by Troncalion. The Forest Guardian fixed Drakkon with an angry stare and gave a low growl at the back of his throat.

Beating his leathery wings, Drakkon touched down ahead of Troncalion and unleashed another blast of searing hot flame. Although the pain was almost unbearable, Troncalion advanced through the fire, keeping his head low as he slowly closed the gap between him and the Volcano Gormiti.

'Ugh, the breath on that thing!' hissed Nick, ducking behind Troncalion to shield himself from the flames.

Toby grinned and made a dash for Drakkon, dodging through the blaze until he was almost level with the creature. 'Time to rinse that mouth!' he

yelled, letting fly with three short water blasts from his claw hand. Each one splashed right to the back of Drakkon's throat, drowning out the fire.

Skidding to a stop, Toby admired his handiwork. Black plumes of smoke curled up from Drakkon's nostrils. He almost cheered. He'd done it – he'd defeated an Ancient Guardian.

Magmion snorted with laughter. 'You can't extinguish the fires of Drakkon, boy!'

Toby saw the first flickering flame reignite in the beast's throat. 'Well,' he gulped, 'it was worth a shot.'

Drakkon reared up onto his hind legs and threw his jaws open wide. Then, just before the first fireball escaped, the dragon's jaws were yanked tightly shut by a long length of forest vine.

'Denied!' cried Lucas, using his forest powers to wrap more and more of the vine around Drakkon's snout, clamping it closed. Drakkon gave an angry hiss, then tossed his head backwards. Still attached to the vines, Lucas was thrown into the air. A second later, he came crashing painfully back down to Earth.

Toby moved to attack once more, only for Drakkon's tail to whip around and slam into his ribs. He tumbled helplessly before Nick's strong stone arms caught him.

Setting Toby down to catch his breath, Nick raced to join Lucas. Troncalion was mounting his own attack on the other Ancient Guardian, using roots and branches from the forest floor to tangle around his feet, tying him to the ground.

'Another feeble attempt to delay the inevitable,' scoffed Magmion, as Drakkon tore free of the trap.

Nick and Lucas charged at the monstrous Volcano Guardian, preparing for the fight of their lives.

But before they could get close, a scorching blast of flame drove them back by its sheer force.

The pain was like nothing they had ever felt before. Despite their great strength, Nick and Lucas dropped to their knees, their hands raised to shield themselves from the heat.

Back in the Primal Pad, Jessica was becoming very worried. 'Glow dropping to critical levels!' she yelped. 'Guys, your orbs are empty!'

Even before Jessica had finished the sentence, Nick and Lucas found themselves back in human form. Their orb energy had been drained away by the heat of Drakkon's flames, and it would be a while before they could change into their Super Gormiti forms again. But as ordinary kids, they had no way of defending themselves!

Unfortunately, this gave Drakkon just the opportunity he was looking for. With a deep breath, the dragon let rip with his most devastating fire attack yet. Nick and Lucas covered their faces, preparing for the end. They didn't see Troncalion move, didn't see him step protectively in front of them. The Guardian howled in pain as he took the full force of the blast.

When the attack finally ended, Troncalion looked up. He was still feeling the effects of Drakkon's attack and every moment brought a new wave of pain. But he would not let the children be hurt. It would take anything Drakkon could deliver, no matter the cost.

It wasn't Drakkon he should have been worried about, though. As Troncalion raised his head, Magmion lashed out with an energy whip. It coiled tightly around Troncalion's throat.

Still weakened, Troncalion could do nothing to resist. He dropped to his knees, gasping for breath, defeated.

Cackling to himself, Magmion yanked the whip away, leaving a gem-studded collar around Troncalion's neck. When Magmion spoke, the gems gave off a strange, eerie glow. Troncalion's eyes shone red as the collar seized control of his mind.

'And now, Troncalion, you belong to Magmion!' the evil Volcano Gormiti laughed. Unable to resist the collar's control, Troncalion slowly got to his feet. Drakkon turned and flapped slowly away, with the Forest Guardian lumbering along behind.

'Today – the Ancients, tomorrow – the world!'
Magmion cried. He turned in his saddle and fixed
Nick and Lucas with a wicked glare. '*Your* world!'

'What does he mean by that?' wondered Nick, as
they watched Troncalion push through the trees in
pursuit of his new master.

'Come on,' urged Lucas, 'we've got to –'

'To what?' asked Toby, who was the only one
of the three to have remained in his Super Gormiti
form. 'You're just a kid, and your pal Trunky isn't
really himself at the moment.'

'His name's Troncalion, and he needs our help!'

Jessica's face appeared in mid-air. 'Which is why
you need to recharge,' she said. 'Toby's still got glow
– he can track them while your orbs glow up.'

Lucas bit his lip, then looked up at Toby. 'Promise
me you'll stick to Magmion like glue.'

Toby rested a powerful hand on his friend's
shoulder. 'By the orbs,' he swore.

Minutes later, Nick and Lucas were back in the
Primal Pad, wishing their powers had held out for
longer. Jessica was on the phone with a frantic Gina.

'There are too many of them,' Gina wailed. 'You
thought escaping zoo animals were wild? You should
see these dogs! I need help, Jessica. Right now, or
I quit. No new dress! No Spring Fling!'

Jessica looked over at the two boys. A smile
lit up her face. Their orbs wouldn't be recharged for
a while yet. It wasn't as if they had anything better
to do.

'OK, don't panic, G,' Jessica grinned. 'Help is
on the way!'

CHAPTER FOUR

THE THIRD GUARDIAN

Gina sat on the grass, wondering how it all could have gone so wrong. Her legs were bound tightly together by a dog lead. The dog itself — a yappy Chihuahua — had run around her in circles, tangling her up until she had fallen over. Now it sat beside her, panting happily, without a care in the world.

Two pairs of hands appeared and caught Gina under the arms. With one sharp pull, they lifted her to her feet and she found herself looking into the smiling faces of Nick and Lucas.

As Nick set to work untangling the lead from around her legs, Lucas asked, 'Are you OK?'

'Oh, hi, Lucas,' said Gina, smiling shyly. 'I'm doing much better ... now that *you're* here.'

'The dogs, Gina,' said Nick impatiently. 'Where are the dogs?'

'You should have seen them,' Gina began to sob. 'Jumping, tugging, barking, licking – it was a nightmare! I'm only one girl ...' She leaned in closer to Lucas and fluttered her eyelashes. '... who's still fielding date offers for the Spring Fling.'

Lucas wasn't paying attention. His eyes were locked on something across the park. 'We've got a woof at twelve o'clock!'

Nick followed his gaze and spotted the dog, sitting beside a bench. Another three dogs sat just beyond it. All four of them eyed the boys suspiciously.

Frantically, Nick and Lucas raced for the dogs, making a grab for their trailing leads. But the dogs sped off, leaving the boys to chase them down.

After twenty minutes of slipping, tripping and tumbling over one another, they finally rounded up all of the runaway dogs. As they walked back over to Gina, they saw her face go pale. The escaped lion – huge, hairy and hungry-looking – was emerging from a nearby bush and roared loudly in her face!

At once, the tiny Chihuahua sprang into action, barking and snapping furiously at the lion. After a moment, the other dogs followed its lead, leaping at the big cat and barking for all they were worth.

Amazingly, the lion began to edge backwards,

startled by the dogs. It was too busy eyeing them to notice the restraining noose slip over its neck. Two uniformed men managed to bundle the furious beast into the back of a reinforced van.

'Great job, kids,' beamed one of the men. 'Are you OK?'

Gina and the boys nodded, too shocked to speak.

'Venture Falls Animal Control,' explained the other man. 'We'll take it from here.'

'S-sure,' stammered Nick. 'Thanks.'

'Wow. Did that just happen?' murmured Gina.

Lucas looked down at the little dog beside Gina. The other dogs had taken their cue from him. It was his barking that had made the others join in and scare away the big cat.

'Wild dogs and a lion in the park ...' he muttered.

'I know,' gasped Gina. 'What could be more exciting than that?'

A short while later, Toby was dealing with some excitement of his own. He was perched high on a cliff overlooking the sea, with Razzle resting on one of his broad shoulders.

'Nicely done, Jessica,' he said, gazing down at the huge, lumbering creature on a narrow strip of sand at the foot of the cliff. 'You really know how to track a magical signature.'

'Troncalion?' Jessica asked, projecting her image from back in the Primal Pad.

'In the flesh,' Toby replied. 'Or ... whatever he is.'

Razzle squinted, studying the beach below. 'What's he doing down there?'

Jessica examined the crystals on the control deck before her. 'I don't know. His magic signature only tells me where he is, not what he's up to.'

An expansive shadow fell across Toby and Razzle. They turned and looked up, and were confronted by a terrible sight.

'Any sign of Magmion and his new pet?' asked Jessica.

Toby swallowed nervously. 'Uh, funny you should ask ...'

Drakkon inhaled and Toby knew he had just

moments to act. Scooping up Razzle, he hurled himself from the cliff, just avoiding a fiery blast.

'Here comes the fun part!' Toby cried, as he plummeted towards the icy sea below. Razzle barely had time to shut his eyes before they both plunged below the surface and out of sight.

Drakkon circled above the waves for a few minutes, searching for any sign of the heroes. When they didn't emerge, Magmion guided the dragon back towards the shore.

'Track me if you like,' he shouted as they flew, 'but there's no sneaking up on Drakkon!'

Far out to sea, Toby's head bobbed up above the surface of the water. He could only just make out the shape of Drakkon in the distance, with Troncalion still standing on the beach just beyond.

'What is he doing out here, anyway?'

Razzle popped up beside him. The little lizard was coughing and spitting out mouthfuls of sea water. 'Aside from ruining my afternoon?'

The sentence was barely out of Razzle's mouth when the water around them began to bubble and froth. 'Huh? Now what?' Toby groaned.

Something large nudged him from below. He looked down just as a gigantic sea creature rose up from the depths beneath him. Razzle leapt onto Toby's back as they were both raised up above the water by an enormous, squid-like beast.

'By the orbs!' squealed Razzle.

Toby had to grip onto the creature's head to stop himself sliding off. As his hands made contact, his body went completely rigid and his eyes glazed over.

'Sea Ancient ...' began Toby. His voice became an excited whisper. 'I think I understand what

Lucas was saying about Trunky. You and me are, like ... we're connected. I'm Toby and you're ...'

He concentrated for a moment. 'Your name is Tentaclion!'

Toby felt the wind in his face and realised Tentaclion was speeding towards the shore. 'You're here to rescue the Ancient Guardian,' Toby said, still reading the creature's thoughts. 'Oh, you mean Trunky!'

Leaping to his feet, Toby rode the giant Tentaclion like a surfboard. 'Yeah,' he cried, 'let's spring Trunky!'

Razzle buried his face in his hands and shook his head. 'Oh boy.'

As they drew closer to the beach, Drakkon swooped around and charged into an attack. 'Come and try it, boy!' screeched Magmion.

Summoning his elemental power, Toby sent tall columns of water rocketing up towards Drakkon. But the Ancient Guardian would not be caught out so easily. He weaved and twisted through the columns, never coming close to touching one. Magmion roared with laughter from the dragon's back.

But Toby wasn't out of ideas yet. As Drakkon flew closer, Toby launched a volley of water globes straight at him. They splattered against the Volcano Gormiti's head, sending him into a spin.

Pulling hard on Drakkon's neck, Magmion managed to steer him away from the water. Toby prepared to attack again, but Magmion had other ideas. With a crack, his magic whip snaked out and coiled around Tentaclion's neck.

'Oh, no, you didn't!' cried Toby, as he realised the Ancient Sea Guardian now wore a collar exactly like Troncalion's. Using his lobster claw, Toby struggled to cut the collar off, but it seemed to be reinforced with magic strength.

As he looked into the sea creature's eyes, they began to glow a dark, sinister shade of red, and Toby knew Tentaclion was now under Magmion's control.

'Uh-oh,' Toby gulped, before the once-friendly beast wrapped a tentacle around his waist and flipped him into the air. He barely had time to see Razzle dive into the water before he was hurled towards the shore, where a large outcrop of deadly, razor-sharp rocks waited to break his fall.

CHAPTER FIVE

BATTLING THE GUARDIANS

Toby screwed his eyes tight shut and waited for the pain to come. It didn't. A split-second before he smashed into the rocks, a net of roots and vines sprang up to catch him.

With an 'oof!' Toby bounced off the net and landed on the soft sand of the beach. He looked up to find Nick and Lucas – back in their Super Gormiti forms – smiling down at him.

'Toby, you're not an Air Gormiti,' Nick grinned. 'Stick to the water where you belong.'

Toby sighed with relief. He'd never been more

glad to see his friends. 'I see you're all charged up and good to glow,' he beamed as Nick helped him up.

A howling wind suddenly whipped up the sand around them. Drakkon hovered above the beach just a few metres away. Each beat of his wings hurled more sand towards the heroes, until they could barely stand.

'I love the ocean,' sniggered Magmion, 'but it's always so windy at the shore!'

Within seconds, Toby, Nick and Lucas were covered in sand from head to toe. Spluttering, Toby shook off the worst of it.

'OK,' he coughed, 'that tanked.'

'Where's Magmion?' asked Nick.

They looked around to find themselves alone on the beach.

'Gone,' Lucas said glumly. 'With the Ancient Guardians.'

A tiny figure dragged itself out of the water and limped over to join them. 'Whew ... OK,' gasped Razzle, fighting to get his breath back after his long swim. 'What did I miss?'

A few minutes later, Lucas, Toby and Nick were climbing up the cliff face, leaving the beach far below. Razzle clung onto Nick's neck, still exhausted from his ordeal in the water.

'We're almost at the top of the ridge,' said Nick. 'How are the readings over there?'

Beside him, the floating image of Jessica shook her head. 'Nuts. Each time Magmion captures one of those big guys, we're seeing bad effects back here on Earth.'

'Rift activity?'

'Tons,' Jessica replied, 'and it's not just animals

going wild any more. Reports of shrivelling forests and of lakes drying up. It's like all the elements of Earth are withering away.'

'We've got to free the Ancients from Magmion's control, and fast,' said Lucas. 'What's he want with them, anyway?'

'And more importantly,' began Toby, 'where exactly are we going?'

'The Cavern of Roscamar is just over the ridge, atop the valley,' Razzle explained.

'The Cavern of Roscamar?' gasped Nick. 'According to legend, that was the last –'

They reached the top of the cliff and found themselves standing in front of a colossal cavern.

'The last known location of the Earth Ancient Guardian,' whispered Razzle.

Lucas peered into the gloom. Nothing appeared to move. 'Bad news. No Ancient Guardian.'

Toby shrugged. 'Good news? No Magmion either.'

'Yeah, tracking his magic signature now,' said Jessica, her projection appearing beside them. 'It's weirdorama. He hasn't moved from the valley.'

The heroes looked down over the cliff. There, far below, was Magmion and the three Ancient Guardians. Something about the way they were just waiting there bothered Nick.

'Toby, Tentaclion emerged from the sea to rescue Troncalion, right?'

'Yeah,' said Toby, 'it was like he knew his Ancient pal was in trouble.'

Lucas realised what Nick was getting at. 'So Magmion doesn't need to find the Earth Ancient, he only needs to bring the Ancients close enough to lure him out.'

He turned to Nick, only to find him standing rigid, staring blankly. 'Uh, Nick?' he said. 'Earth to Nick?'

'The Ancient,' said Nick. 'He's close. I can feel it.'

Razzle looked around. 'He's here?'

With a sound like grinding stone, an eye flicked open on the wall of the cavern. The whole inside of the cave began to move, as the Earth Ancient broke free from his hiding place.

'Yes,' cheered Nick. 'And his name is Roscalion!'

Roscalion exploded from inside the cave like a giant charging rhino. The entire mountain shook as the huge, stony-skinned beast thundered towards the cliff edge, billowing around him as he ran.

'Whoa!' Nick yelped, as Roscalion leapt off the edge. 'I'm telling him to stop, but he's too desperate to help the others to listen.'

'Then it's our destiny to help, too!' cried Lucas.

'Destiny?' spluttered Razzle. 'I just realised we're in Destiny Valley – the most magically charged place in Gorm!'

Jessica's worried face appeared in the air beside them. 'Guys, I did some cross-referencing in some scrolls and I've got bad news. The Earthbound rifts we're seeing are symptoms of a portal opening – Magmion is trying to enter Earth!'

The heroes didn't need to hear any more. Throwing themselves off the cliff edge, they crashed down onto the beach, ready for battle.

Magmion was waiting for them, still sitting astride Drakkon. Nick reeled in horror as he realised Roscalion had already been snared by one of the control collars.

'Four Ancients in Destiny Valley,' Magmion hissed. Behind him, swirls of magical energy swept up from within the Ancients into the sky and combined to form a vast hole in space. 'A culmination of power to make a portal to your world! I can't wait to see what it's like ... so I can *destroy* it!'

Toby, Nick and Lucas moved to charge at him, but the Guardians blocked their way. 'Go on,' Magmion laughed. 'Try to stop me!'

'Uh, guys, even *you* are no match for the combined power of the Ancients,' Razzle whimpered.

'It's not the Ancients we want,' replied Toby, his eyes still fixed on Magmion.

'Hurry, guys,' warned Jessica. 'The portal is expanding!'

'We've got to free them from those collars,' Nick barked, as the Ancients closed in around them.

'Easier said than done,' replied Toby. 'I already tried cutting it off.'

Lucas moved his gaze across the gathered Guardians. Troncalion, Tentaclion and Roscalion all seemed to be following Drakkon's lead. It was as if they were watching him, waiting for him to tell them exactly what to do next. Their behaviour reminded of something – but what?

'It's like the dogs in the park,' Lucas realised. 'One is leading the others. If we destroy Drakkon's collar, it might deactivate the other collars.'

There was no time to discuss the plan further. The Ancients lunged forwards, and it was all the boys could do to avoid being trampled underfoot. Toby ran up Troncalion's back and bounced on the Guardian's moss-covered head. With a roar of effort, he sent a water orb arcing towards Drakkon's long, thin neck.

KZZZZT!

As the ball of spinning water hit, the collar began to spark furiously. With a crackle of electricity, it unclipped and fell towards the ground. Nick made a desperate dive for the falling collar and brought his solid stone fists smashing down on it with all his might.

Magmion looked at the other Guardians warily. In unison, their collars clicked open and fell to the ground, and the red glow faded from their eyes. Above them, the portal to Earth shrank shut, then disappeared completely.

'My Ancients!' he howled. 'You totally stole my Ancients!

Lucas, Toby and Nick all climbed onto the backs of their elemental cousins.

'The Ancients don't belong to you or anyone,' Nick called.

'No, but my lava steed is still loyal to me!' Magmion screeched, as he steered Drakkon back towards the Volcano Nation. 'One of these days,

Lords of Nature, I will learn all your secrets. And when I do, you will bow to me!'

The boys watched as Magmion fled, then looked at each other and shrugged.

'What a weirdo,' Toby muttered.

Less than an hour later, the friends were all back in human form, and gathered outside Jessica's house.

'That's a pretty good haul for a day of dog walking,' Jessica said. She shared the money out among the others and groaned. 'Until you split it five ways.'

'There's barely enough for make-up, much less a dress and shoes,' said Gina in dismay.

They leapt back as a van screeched to a halt beside them. The back doors flew open and a young woman with a microphone jumped out.

'Excuse me, you're the kids that fought off that lion in the park today, right?' she asked.

Lucas nodded. 'Uh, yeah.'

'I'd like to pay you for an exclusive interview!'

Nick almost choked. 'Seriously?'

Jessica's phone buzzed in her pocket. 'Hello?' she said, snapping it open. 'Oh sorry, no, we're officially out of the dog walking business.' She looked at her friends and smiled. 'We're getting into television!'

Gina and Jessica exchanged an excited high-five. Beside them, the three boys laughed happily. It looked like they'd be getting that advance release of Skull Blasters 8000, after all. They could only hope that the world of Gorm stayed safe long enough for them to play it!

Beastly

Lucas meets Troncalion,
the Forest Ancient Guardian

Magmion and his dragon steed, Drakkon

Nick and Lucas rescue Gina

Tentaclion gives Toby and Razzle a wet ride

The Ancient Guardians fall under an evil spell

Magmion captures Roscalion

Toby launches a water blast

Nick causes an earthquake

Keeper Kept

Nick, Lucas and Jessica fall
under Firespitter's trance

Nick prepares to attack his brother

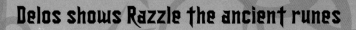

Delos shows Razzle the ancient runes

Jessica's tornado exposes the ocean floor

Jessica and Lucas lose their powers while fighting Helico the Wary.

Nick transforms underwater, and is saved by Toby

Firespitter and Crabs topple into the ocean

Toby makes a wish on
the Lost Heart of Desire

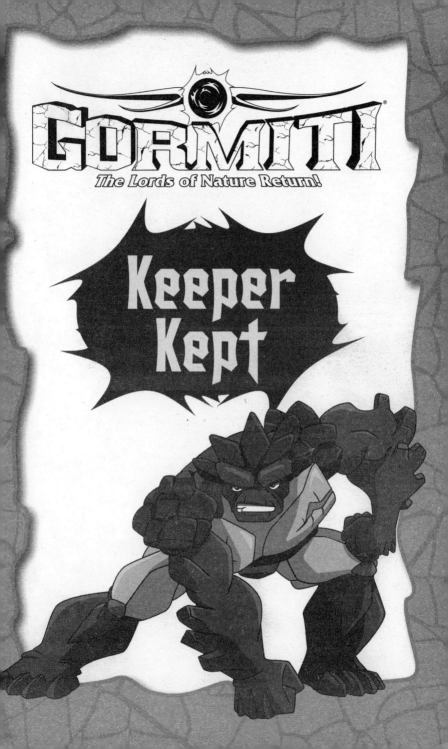

CONTENTS

CHAPTER ONE

WASH OUT

It was early morning in Venture Falls, and the subway station was packed with people heading for work. Rows of commuters waited impatiently by the track, listening to the clackety-clack of the train as it sped through the underground tunnel.

The train's headlights appeared in the darkness, but it was clear that something was wrong. The train was moving much too fast to stop. With a whoosh of wind, it flew right past the station and disappeared into the mouth of the tunnel at the far end.

The passengers glanced at each other, confused. Then they heard it – another sound, echoing along the tunnel from which the train had just emerged. Was it another train? No, this sound wasn't the rattle of wheels on the track. It was more like ... a roar.

The roar of rushing water!

Screaming, the passengers abandoned their bags and briefcases and ran for the stairs, as a torrent of water swept down the tracks and crashed onto the platform.

Everyone in the station clambered up the steps to the surface. As the final few passengers dragged themselves up, the water had already risen to street level. It seeped out onto the pavement, soaking the shoes of a TV journalist, who was the first reporter on the scene.

All around the reporter, manhole covers popped open and flipped up like pancakes in the air as the

pressure of the water below forced them upwards.
In moments, the entire street was flooded.

'It's a miracle that no one was injured,' the news
reporter said, speaking into the camera. 'Is it
an underground well? Broken water main? City
officials say "no". It's as though two thousand gallons
of sea water just appeared from thin air!'

Nick gritted his teeth. He wasn't backing down on
this. 'Is not!' he snapped.

'Is too!' replied a blond boy who stood several centimetres taller than Nick. Ike Pinkney was a rich kid who thought his parents' money gave him the right to push people around and behave in any way he liked. This didn't make him very popular with most of the other kids in school.

The boys were in the classroom where Nick's after-school archaeology club took place every week. Around them, ten other students – including Nick's friends, Jessica and Gina – watched the argument in silence.

'But we're archaeologists!' Nick cried.

'No, we're a junior high school club. There's a big difference,' insisted Ike.

Nick held up a magazine and jabbed a finger against a picture of a clay vase on the front. 'Not if we start a real dig and find a real three-handled Hoachi pot.'

Snatching the magazine from Nick's hand, Ike rolled it into a tight tube. He looked at Nick through it, as if through a telescope at some distant planet. 'Earth to Nick,' he snorted, 'real archaeologists had digs all up and down the Grand River, and do you know how many Hoachi pots they found? Zero.'

'So your plan is to blow our club funds on pizza?' Nick shook his head in disgust.

'And soda,' Ike added.

Jessica clapped with excitement. 'Ooh, soda!' she trilled. She stopped when Nick flashed her an angry look. 'Oh, sorry,' she mumbled. 'Just ... thirsty.'

'Look, the only reason you're president of this club is because you started it, right?' asked Ike, prodding Nick with his finger.

'Yeah, and the only reason you're here is because it's easy extra credit,' Nick replied.

'Sure,' Ike admitted, before turning to Gina. 'But aren't all school clubs supposed to elect their officials?'

'Technically, yes,' Gina said.

Ike pulled out a chair and stood on it. He turned to address all the gathered students. 'Then I, Ike Pinkney, am officially running for club president.' He pointed down at Nick. 'I challenge you to a club debate. The winner gets to be president!'

'You can't do that!' Nick gasped. He turned to Gina and whispered, 'Can he do that?'

Gina shrugged apologetically. 'Technically,' she said, 'yes.'

An hour later, Nick was on the back step of his house, his head in his hands. His friends, Lucas and Jessica, were in the garden, along with his older brother, Toby. As Nick sat there feeling sorry for himself, the others were hard at work making posters urging people to vote for him in the debate.

'I wish I could just be president of my own archaeology club without having to win a stupid debate,' Nick grumbled.

'Don't sweat it, bro,' said Lucas, encouragingly. 'No one's going to vote for Ike.'

Jessica actually seemed disappointed at that. 'But if you win, we'll have to dig through dirt and stuff,' she said, shuddering at the thought of the damage that would do to her nails.

'It's an *archaeology* club!' Nick yelled, leaping to his feet.

'Hey, I'm here helping you, aren't I?' Jessica scowled. She turned to her picture and deliberately went outside the lines with her paintbrush.

'So,' asked Toby, 'when is this "big debate"?'

'Tonight,' Nick answered gloomily.

'Well, you've got my vote!' chimed a voice.

Nick yelped with fright at the sudden appearance of Razzle, the talking lizard. Startled, Razzle also let out a scream and leapt a metre into the air. He was still yowling when he landed on Jessica's shoulder, and ducked for cover behind her head.

'Hey, Razzle,' she said. 'Trouble in Gorm?'

He nodded. 'Would I be here if there wasn't?'

Nick and Toby's mum and dad stood beside the hob, watching the contents of a pot bubble and boil. Giving the liquid a stir, Mum scooped up a spoonful and held it up for Dad to taste.

SCHLURP!

'Mmm,' said Dad. 'Decadently delicious!'

The adults were so busy with their tasting session, they failed to notice the four children sneak into the room behind them.

'Your parents are such a pain,' Jessica said in a low whisper. 'I wish they didn't spend so much time in the kitchen.'

'Tippy toes, people,' warned Nick, as he led the way across to the kitchen pantry, where the secret doorway leading down to the Primal Pad lay.

The kids kept low as they snuck over to the pantry door. Mum and Dad began to turn, but Toby and the others quickly bundled into the pantry just before they were spotted.

Inside the little cupboard, they each swept their hands across the hidden scanner. A large section of the floor began to sink downwards in segments, forming a long flight of stairs.

With Razzle leading the way, the four friends hurried down the steps, only stopping when they reached the Primal Pad – the control room where they could look through the Gorm Gate down at the world of Gorm.

Razzle wasted no time in getting down to business. 'The Sea Gormiti of the southern coast are causing tectonic instability along their own coastline,' he said.

An image appeared in the Gorm Gate of a rocky shore. A moment later, it changed to show a subway station filling with water.

'Whatever they're doing caused the flooding in Venture Falls' subway earlier today,' Razzle explained.

Toby grinned. 'Subway surfing, anyone?'

'Don't laugh,' Razzle snapped. His little face was deadly serious. 'If the Sea Gormiti aren't stopped, this is just the beginning. Your entire city could be washed right off the map!'

The children exchanged worried looks. They hurried over to the four elemental orbs – Earth, Water, Air and Forest – placed around the Gorm Gate. Together, they recited the chant that would reveal the Keeper.

'And the Keeper is ...' Razzle paused as the Keeper's chair spun round and round. When it came to a stop, an aqua-blue icon was displayed on its back.

'... Sea!'

Toby groaned. 'Aw, man. I hate being stuck in the Primal Pad.'

He shuffled over to the chair and slumped down into it. When he did, the seat rose magically into the air, lifting him up until he was sitting directly in front of a control panel made up of hundreds of long, thin crystals.

'I wish I could be in Gorm where all the action is,' he complained, fiddling with a few of the crystals. As he slid the final crystal into place, the Gorm Gate began to ripple like water.

The three other children stepped up onto the stone edge of the portal. They each took a deep breath, steadied their nerves, then jumped through.

With a splash, they passed through the portal and the three of them – with Razzle by their side – tumbled down towards the mysterious land of Gorm.

CHAPTER TWO

HYPNOTISED

Lucas, Jessica and Nick touched gently down on the ground. Razzle wasn't so graceful, thudding against a rock and tumbling onto the sand.

Toby consulted the pages of a heavy book, then projected his image to the team in Gorm. 'The Travel Tome says you're at the Beach of the Lonely Escape,' he told them.

The children looked around. Dozens of Sea Gormiti were filing out of the water, almost bent double beneath the weight of the heavy boulders they carried on their shoulders. As they struggled out of the water, more Gormiti walked in to take their place.

'Why would someone want to escape?' Lucas muttered. 'This place looks like loads of fun.'

'Excuse me. Um, hello?' said Jessica, trying to attract the attention of the Gormiti. *Hello?*

The blue-skinned figures continued to march past her, unspeaking. Even Crabs the Avenger – a heroic Sea Gormiti they had met in the past – ignored her.

'Rude much?' she scowled.

Razzle clambered up onto Nick's shoulder. 'I don't know, kids,' he fretted. 'I'm getting the spooky-ookies here.'

They watched the line of rock-carriers make their way to a large archway, where another Sea Gormiti was using a larger stone to smash the collected rocks into dust. But there was something unsettling about the way the Gormiti were moving. Their steps were almost robotic, all walking at the same slow, methodical pace.

As each rock was smashed, yet another Gormiti would dig through the pebbles and grit as if searching for something.

'What are they looking for?' Lucas wondered.

Before the others could answer, a large shadow fell over them. Up in the Primal Pad, a warning light on Toby's control panel began to flash red.

'Uh, guys,' he said. 'There are signs of a Volcano Gormiti in your area! Better keep an eye out.'

At this, the children whipped around to find themselves staring at a giant, bulbous eyeball. It had a blood-red pupil and was positioned right in the middle of the face of Firespitter, an evil Volcano Gormiti. With a yelp of fear, Razzle darted for cover, hiding inside a seashell.

'Gaze into my eye!' the red-skinned Gormiti commanded. Flames seemed to dance in the middle of his enormous pupil as he worked his hypnotic powers on the children. 'You cannot resist the will of Firespitter!'

It was over in less than a minute. Unable to resist Firespitter's hypnotic stare, Lucas, Nick and Jessica fell into a deep trance, their eyes glazing over and their mouths flopping open mindlessly.

'You will do as I command,' boomed the

Volcano Gormiti. 'And I command you to ...' He paused, thinking hard. '... make me a sandwich!' he demanded.

Obeying, Lucas, Nick and Jessica shambled off to find some bread. 'No! Wait! There is no time for snacks!' Firespitter decided. 'You will join the others in the search!'

Nodding slowly, the kids shuffled across to join the Sea Gormiti. Razzle watched them plod, zombie-like, across the sand. 'I think we have a problem,' he muttered to himself.

In the Primal Pad, Toby checked the magic orbs, which gave the team the power to change into their Gormiti alter egos. 'Orbs are charged and good to glow,' he reported. 'The team can transform at will.'

'No they can't!' Razzle hissed. 'This lava loon's giving them the evil eye.'

Toby's flickering image appeared next to the lizard. 'What do you mean?'

'I mean they've gone all zombie!'

'Well, I'm stuck here in the Primal Pad,' Toby reminded him. 'What do you want me to do?'

'Something! *Anything!*' cried Razzle.

Toby lowered his head in frustration. The others were in danger and he was stuck up here, messing about with crystals.

'Razzle's right,' he said aloud. Activating the Gorm Gate, he jumped down from the chair. 'Keeper or no Keeper, it's up to me!'

He raced over to the portal, hopped up onto the

ledge, then launched himself through the gate's
shimmering surface.

As he tumbled through the clouds high above
Gorm, Toby said the words that would transform
him into his powerful Gormiti form.

'Elemental powers flow,' he yelled into the wind,
'Gormiti, Lords of Nature, go!'

Toby continued to fall, but as he did, an amazing
transformation took place. By the time he landed on
the ground, Toby – the boy – had gone. In his place
was Toby the Super Gormiti, boasting all the
powers of the sea.

Almost at once, Toby spotted the others. They were walking along the beach, carrying large rocks. They walked in perfect formation, side by side, their footsteps falling at exactly the same time.

Toby took cover behind a rock, then leaned out so only the children could see him. 'Guys,' he hissed. 'Uh, guys?'

Lucas, Nick and Jessica all turned their heads at once. They seemed to look right at Toby, but then turned away and continued walking. Toby shuddered when he saw their blank, emotionless expressions.

He opened his mouth to call them again, but a sudden roar from behind cut him short.

'Behold!' bellowed Firespitter, catching Toby by the shoulder and spinning him round. 'Gaze into my hypnotic eye!'

Gasping, Toby tried to pull away, but already the evil Gormiti's power was taking effect. Try as he might, Toby couldn't move. In a moment, he would be completely under Firespitter's control.

'Not you, too! Snap out of it, kid,' wailed Razzle, scurrying across the sand and leaping up onto Toby's shoulders. He caught hold of his long, tentacle-like hair and used it to cover Toby's eyes.

Firespitter snarled and extended a finger in the little lizard's direction. A stream of steaming lava shot from his fingertip, missing Razzle by mere millimetres.

'Never try to block my eye,' Firespitter warned.

Toby pushed his hair back out of his eyes. Razzle's quick thinking had bought him enough time to come to his senses. He was no longer under Firespitter's control.

'Yeah?' he snapped. 'Well, never mess with my friends!'

A series of icy-cold water globes shot from Toby's stomach. They slammed into Firespitter, sending the villain stumbling backwards.

'You have no friends here,' Firespitter seethed, holding up his hands to block the onrushing water. He looked across the beach to where his slaves were still hard at work. 'Get him!' he commanded.

At once, the Sea Gormiti dropped their rocks and began advancing on Toby. 'Get him,' they droned

in low, monotone voices. 'Get him.'

Lucas, Nick and Jessica closed in on Toby, too.
As they drew closer, their bodies began to glow with
a magical light. Toby groaned. He knew what was
coming next.

'Elemental forces flow,' said the three children,
their voices empty of all emotion. 'Gormiti, Lords
of Nature, go.'

Before Toby's eyes, the trio transformed into their
Super Gormiti forms. Jessica grew a pair of large,
bird-like wings as she became the Lord of Air.

Nick's body doubled in size and hardened into stone, changing into the super-strong Lord of Earth.

Moss and vines sprouted all over Lucas. His muscles bulged and grew as he transformed into the Lord of Forest.

They stared at Toby with glazed eyes, as if they didn't even recognise their teammate.

'Get Toby,' they said dully, and slowly began to advance.

'*Eye* like what *eye* see!' giggled Firespitter.

Toby gave a heavy sigh. 'This,' he muttered, as Razzle leapt from his shoulder and scampered back to the safety of a seashell, 'just keeps getting better.'

CHAPTER THREE

DESTROY THE KEEPER

The ground beneath Toby's feet began to tremble and quake. He looked down in time to see a dozen plant vines sprout from the sand and snake up his legs. Kicking furiously, he fought to be free, but it was no use. Lucas's vines had him trapped.

With a wave of his hand, Lucas made the vines whip Toby into a nearby cliff face. Toby cried out in pain as his back smashed hard against the rough stone.

There was no time to recover. Nick lunged, swinging a mighty rock fist at his brother's head.

Toby ducked just in time as Nick punched a hole deep into the cliff. As Nick struggled to pull himself free, Toby wrapped his tentacles around his brother's body and tossed him back towards Lucas.

CRUNCH!

Nick's heavy stone body smashed into Lucas, their heads cracking as they crashed to the ground. For a moment, their eyes seemed to spin crazily. The two Super Gormiti exchanged a confused look. What was going on?

Still under the trance, Jessica launched into the sky. Summoning the power of the wind, she blasted a powerful gust down at Toby. Dust and sand were churned up, knocking Toby over. The howling wind and the sand stung Toby's eyes, forcing him to shut them tight. He didn't see Firespitter approach, his eye blazing with hypnotic power.

'Open your eyes,' the Volcano Gormiti hissed, 'and accept your fate!'

In response, Lucas transformed his hand into brown, plant-like vines and coiled them around Firespitter's head, covering his eye completely.

'Get this off me!' Firespitter screeched, as the vines wrapped him from head to toe.

Nick, meanwhile, was helping his brother to his feet. 'Toby, what are you doing here?' he demanded.

'Saving your butts,' Toby replied.

Lucas staggered as a blast of hurricane-force wind hit him, forcing him to release his grip on Firespitter, who fell, face-first, onto the sand.

Then a mini-tornado whipped up around Lucas,

spinning him around and around until he collapsed, dizzy, to the ground. He had a good idea where it was coming from ...

Jessica flew near, bearing down on the fallen Lucas.

Summoning his sea powers, Toby shot an enormous water globe up towards her. As the icy water struck, she dropped from the sky like a stone.

Just before she hit the ground, her wings opened and she lifted back into the air. She looked down on the scene below her, with no idea of what had just happened.

'Toby?' she gasped, amazed to see that the Keeper wasn't in the Primal Pad.

'Aaargh!' roared Firespitter. He clambered to his feet, clawing at his face. 'Sand in the eye!' he howled. He gestured wildly to where the children were gathered. 'Destroy them! Destroy them!'

Like a giant swarm, the Sea Gormiti all moved as one. At first, they walked slowly towards the children, but soon, they broke into a run. There were dozens of them. Hundreds, maybe. Far too many to fight.

Besides, the Lords didn't want to hurt the Sea Gormiti. It wasn't their fault that Firespitter was controlling them.

'This could get real ugly, real fast,' said Nick. A blast of lava streaked through the air towards him, as Firespitter joined the chase. There was nothing else for it, the heroes realised – they had to run!

'Let's ditch 'em over there,' cried Lucas, making for a maze of rocks and caves which stood just a few hundred metres away.

As they sprinted along the beach, Toby took a detour past the shell that Razzle was hiding in. Not slowing, he reached down and caught hold of the little lizard and sat him on his shoulder. They ran fast, but the Sea Gormiti were running faster. The gap between them was closing ... fast!

A burst of lava made the sand behind Toby explode. The blast launched him into the air, forcing Razzle to cling on for dear life. Lucas and Nick both caught hold of one of Toby's legs, trying to stop him soaring too high. They were shocked to discover that their combined weight didn't slow him. He just kept going up and up and up!

Nick looked up and realised why. Jessica was holding onto Toby's arms and using all her strength to fly the whole team towards a cave, high on a nearby cliff. Gritting her teeth, Jessica flew higher. Muscles straining, she managed to drag the boys up to the cave, before her grip slipped and they tumbled down onto the rocky ground outside the cave mouth.

Far below, they heard Firespitter roar with rage, and the footsteps of the Sea Gormiti stumble to a stop.

'That should buy us some time,' Jessica smiled, landing softly beside her friends. Her arms and wings were aching, but she had saved them all. For now.

Suddenly, a blue tentacle coiled around her and squeezed tight, cutting off her air. Lucas, Nick and Toby tensed, ready to fight. The Sea Gormiti holding Jessica raised a large claw and snipped the air right beside his prisoner's head.

'Don't even think it,' he growled.

'Step down, Delos,' said a voice. Another Sea Gormiti stepped from the mouth of a cave. She was larger than Delos, with razor-sharp fins on her arms and legs. 'These Gormiti resisted Firespitter's spell,' she said. Despite her scary appearance, the female Sea Gormiti's voice was wise and soothing.

Nick raised a rocky eyebrow. 'I see we're not the only ones.'

'It pains me to see our people twisted to Firespitter's will,' she said. Without another word, she turned and walked back into the cave.

'Come,' urged Delos, beckoning them with his tentacle arm, 'it is not safe in the open.'

Following Delos, the children entered the cave, with Razzle scurrying along behind. As soon as they were inside, a large rock magically rolled across the entrance, blocking their only way out.

Stepping out from his hiding place near the cave, Crabs the Avenger gave a low, menacing laugh.

The two mysterious Sea Gormiti led the team into a vast cavern. Blue light flickered and danced across the walls, reflecting off a deep pool that lay in the centre of the room.

Mantra, the female Sea Gormiti, stood gazing into the water and began to explain what she knew. 'Firespitter is searching for the Lost Heart of Desire,' she said.

'Is that like a romance novel?' Jessica guessed.

Delos drew in a deep breath. 'It is an ancient amulet of powerful magic. The runes say it was lost on this very shore.'

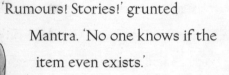

'Rumours! Stories!' grunted Mantra. 'No one knows if the item even exists.'

Delos reached out with his tentacle and gave Toby a pat on the shoulder. 'You're lucky your friend came when he did,' he said. 'Firespitter's spell was still new and weak enough to break.'

Toby grinned and held out his arms. 'Am I your hero or what?'

'You're supposed to be our Keeper,' Jessica reminded him.

'Yeah,' said Lucas, angrily. 'How do we get back without a Keeper running the Gorm Gate?'

Nick grabbed his brother by the shoulders. 'And how am I going to defend my club presidency against Ike if I'm a rock man on the shores of Gorm?' he cried.

Even though he'd saved them all, Toby found himself feeling bad. 'That silly club really means a lot to you, doesn't it?' he asked Nick in disbelief.

Nick nodded. 'It does, and if I'm a no-show at the debate, then Ike will be president.'

'I'm not going to let that happen,' Toby promised. 'We'll think of something.'

'We'd better think fast,' said Lucas. 'Without a Keeper to charge our orbs, we're going to run out of power soon. And when we do, we're going to be normal human kids in a heap of Gorm trouble!'

CHAPTER FOUR

THE ANCIENT RUNES

Nick turned to Delos and Mantra. 'What runes were you talking about?'

The two Sea Gormiti glanced at each other, then nodded. With a wave of her hand, Mantra guided the heroes towards a stone door at the back of the cave.

The door led through to a small room. Strange hieroglyphics had been carved into the walls. As they entered, a faint orange light from the setting sun crept in through a crack in the rock wall. All around them, the carvings began to glow an eerie shade of green.

'The morning Firespitter infiltrated this
chamber was the beginning of the end for my
people,' Mantra told them sadly.

'Whoa!' gasped Razzle, as more of the runes lit
up across the ceiling.

'Yes, this only happens at sunset,' Delos said,
motioning towards the slice of orange light. 'Can
you make out any of the markings?'

Nick crossed to the closest wall and brushed his
hand across it. 'They're old Narlik water runes!'
he said, excitedly.

'Well done,' replied Delos, impressed. 'We can barely decipher the ancient text ourselves.'

'I studied a tome of these back in the Primal Pad.'

Jessica rolled her eyes and whispered to Toby and Lucas, 'Why am I not surprised?'

'No wonder Firespitter wants the amulet,' Nick said, translating some of the runes. 'It's like a genie stone.'

Toby's eyes widened with surprise. 'As in three wishes?'

'We could wish our way home,' said Nick, nodding.

'We could stop Firespitter!' added Lucas.

Jessica bounced up and down with excitement

and smiled at Mantra. 'We could save your tribe!'

Mantra gave a snort of disbelief and turned to Nick. 'If the amulet truly exists, then why hasn't Firespitter found it by now?'

Nick scanned another section of wall, reading the glowing runes. A broad smile spread across his face. 'Because he's digging in the wrong place!'

Mantra looked at him curiously. 'How do you know this, Earth Gormiti?'

Nick turned to face the female Sea Gormiti. 'You said Firespitter was in this chamber during the morning. These runes only appear at sunset, so he wouldn't have seen them!' Nick explained excitedly. 'And without the full set of instructions given in these runes, he doesn't know where to dig.'

Mantra thought for a moment, then gave a single, slow nod of her head. 'If this proves to be true, then your archaeology skills are most impressive.'

Nick shrugged his shoulders in frustration. 'Tell that to Ike Pinkney!'

At that very moment, Ike was sitting at the front of the classroom, facing the assembled members of the archaeology club. He glanced at his watch, then sprang to his feet.

'Nick is too scared to show his face, or he'd be here by now,' he crowed.

'So he's running a little late ...' said Gina.

Ike snorted. 'It's been over an hour!'

He held up a book for the others to see. 'According to the school charter, if the opponent does not show up for the presidential debate, then he or she forfeits the right to stand.'

'Congratulations, Ike,' said Gina. 'You can read.'

'I can read that Nick blew it,' Ike grinned, tossing the book aside. 'Now I, Ike Pinkney, am the new president!' He cleared his throat noisily. 'For my first decree as president ...' he began.

'Pizza and sodas?' sighed Gina.

'Even better. I'm kicking a certain member out of my archaeology club!' Ike said, laughing wickedly. 'Nick Tripp is finished!'

Ike leaned against the desk, sniggering at the nastiness of his own plan. 'I can't wait to see the look on Tripp's face when he learns that I banned him from his own club.'

'You can't do that,' said Gina, standing up.

'Why not? I'm the president, right?'

Gina snatched up the book that Ike had dropped, flipped frantically through it, then smiled as she held up a page for him to see. 'According to your precious school charter, you can't win the debate until you've stated your case.'

Ike hesitated, then shrugged and pulled out his speech. 'Fine,' he said. 'There are many reasons you should vote for Ike instead of that lame-o Nick Tripp. Let me count the ways.'

He let the long piece of paper unfurl. By the time it had fully opened, Ike's speech reached all the way down to the floor.

Relieved, Gina slid back into her seat and peered

out of the window at the darkening sky. 'Come on, Nick,' she whispered. 'Where are you?'

Jessica stood twenty metres from the shore, the sea water lapping around her waist. She held up her hands and closed her eyes. If this was going to work, it would take all her concentration and power.

A tornado whipped up around her. Faster and faster it spun, until the water was sucked up into a spinning spout, leaving her standing in a circle of dry land.

From the cliff high above, Crabs the Avenger watched Jessica's impressive trick. Firespitter had sent him to spy on the heroes, in case they tried to mount an attack. It didn't look like they were attacking, but they were definitely up to something. Crabs turned and shuffled back to where the other brainwashed Sea Gormiti were hard at work. Whatever the four strange Super Gormiti were up to, Firespitter must be told.

'We don't have all day,' Jessica said through clenched teeth. 'This is really taking the wind out of me.'

Lucas, Nick and Toby pushed their way through the tower of water and joined Jessica in the clearing.

'Now,' said Nick, changing his hands into spinning stone drills, 'let's see what we can find.'

Driving his hands down against the seabed, he began to drill through the rock, until a sharp pain stopped him. As Nick watched, his drill hands glowed with magical energy. He realised in horror that his energy orb must be drained. In a flash, he changed back into human form.

Perched on a rock near by, Mantra and Delos gasped with wonder. 'By the lords of the sea! What manner of magic changes powerful Gormiti into puny weaklings?' they wondered.

'Oh, no!' said Jessica.

'Out of glow!' cried Lucas, staring down at the all-too-human Nick.

'Just dig,' said Nick, urgently. 'We've got to find that amulet so we can get the jump on Firespitter.'

'I wouldn't count on it!' boomed a familiar voice. Firespitter stood on a rocky outcrop, glaring down at the group. 'Now, who should finish off these Gormiti pests?'

A hulking brute with drills for arms stepped

up to join him. 'I know,' Firespitter smirked. 'Helico the Wary!'

Taking his cue, the brainwashed Sea Gormiti dived from the cliff towards the heroes. As he fell, his drill arms began to spin so fast, they were little more than a deadly blur.

The children leapt out of the way just before Helico landed. His arms bore into the ground, sending rocks and chunks of debris in all directions.

Jessica took to the air, trying to avoid the flying rocks. As she soared above the ground, her wings began to glow and she felt her powers fade.

'Talk about lousy timing,' she wailed, finding herself back as a human once more. 'A little help?' she shouted, as she plummeted towards the ground.

'Creeper catch!' bellowed Lucas, extending his vines and catching Jessica in mid-fall. Jessica smiled, but her relief didn't last long. With a flash, Lucas's power orb drained and he, too, found himself back as a normal boy.

With an 'oof!', Jessica crashed down on top of Lucas, knocking him to the ground.

With an explosion of stone, Helico blasted up from beneath the seabed . Up on the clifftop, Firespitter clapped with excitement as the hypnotised Sea Gormiti raised his deadly drills and closed in on the helpless children.

CHAPTER FIVE

GOING UNDER

A thunderous noise stopped Helico in his tracks. He turned to see the towering water spout come crashing down, no longer held up by Jessica's powers. Nick, Lucas and Jessica barely had time to take a breath before the water swirled over them and dragged them below the surface.

Luckily, Toby hadn't yet changed back. Still in his Gormiti form, he swam with powerful strokes

through the swirling waves. Reaching out with his tentacle-like hair, he caught his friends before they could sink any further.

Jessica, Lucas and Nick – who had managed to grab hold of Razzle before the waves had hit – gulped down huge mouthfuls of air as they were thrown up to the surface.

SPLASH!

'There are times,' wheezed Jessica, 'when a girl really needs her hairdryer.'

The still surface beside them was broken by two squirming figures, rocketing up from the depths below. Toby and Helico were locked in battle. Helico had his arms out and was spinning like helicopter blades. It was all Toby could do to avoid being sliced to ribbons.

Then, with another splash, they both dropped back down below the waves and sunk out of sight.

Mantra and Delos had sat on the sidelines for too long. They launched themselves towards the water. As they vanished below the surface, Nick, Jessica, Lucas and Razzle were left alone.

Or, almost alone. Up on the cliffs, Firespitter and Crabs the Avenger were watching on. They were too far away for the children to hear what they were saying, but Firespitter looked angry.

A sudden squeal from Jessica made the boys turn in the water. 'Ewww!' she squealed, pulling what looked like a thick, green rope from her hair. 'Seaweed!'

Lucas looked at the water around Jessica. Long lengths of slimy seaweed floated on the surface.

That gave Lucas an idea.

'Eye-boy is going to pay!' he muttered.

Under the sea, Toby, Mantra and Delos were bravely trying to take on Helico. The brainwashed Gormiti's spinning drill arms made it impossible to get close, however, and it was taking all their agility to avoid getting hurt.

Helico swam down towards Toby, thrusting his drills out before him. Toby pushed off from the seabed with his flipper-like feet, moving out

of harm's way and sending Helico slamming against the rocky floor.

The water turned murky as Helico's drills punched a hole through the rock. Toby could hardly believe his eyes when he spotted a glittering golden object come floating up towards him. The amulet!

Swimming towards it, Toby stretched out a hand. But before he could grab the amulet, his body began to glow. As his sea powers faded, Toby found himself desperately short on air.

There was no time to get the amulet. If he didn't make it to the surface right away, he would drown! Kicking frantically, he raced upwards, his face turning purple as he struggled to keep his mouth closed.

With a great gasp, Toby's head popped free of the water. All he could do was tread water and hope that the other Sea Gormiti could get to the amulet before Helico did.

Up on the cliff, Firespitter was becoming more and more agitated. 'What's going on down there? I can't see anything!' He shoved Crabs angrily. 'Kind

of ironic, I've got this giant eye and yet I can't see.
Know what I mean?'

'You don't know the half of it!' came a voice from
below.

Firespitter leaned over the edge and looked down
curiously, just as a slimy seaweed lasso looped over
his head and tightened across his face.

Another length of seaweed wrapped around
Crabs' foot. He stared down at it and gulped. 'Uh-oh.'

'The bigger they are ...' Jessica said sweetly. She
and Nick were holding onto the seaweed rope that
was now attached to Crabs.

'... the harder they fall,' finished Nick, and
together they began to pull.

On another rock just a few metres away, Toby and Lucas heaved on the seaweed they had used to snare Firespitter. Although the two Gormiti were stronger than the children, Lucas and the others had the element of surprise on their side. With one big tug, they yanked the Gormiti off the cliff and cheered as the villains plunged into the icy water below.

As Firespitter and Crabs sunk down, Mantra bobbed up. Toby smiled when he realised what the female Sea Gormiti was holding – the amulet! Winding back her arm, Mantra tossed the amulet over to Nick, who caught it easily.

'The Lost Heart of Desire,' growled Firespitter, dragging his soaking body up onto a rock. 'Give it to me, or I'll ...'

He pointed his fingers at Toby, ready to hit him with deadly lava blasts. But instead of searing hot fire, only cold sea water trickled out of the Volcano Gormiti's finger holes.

A large ocean wave suddenly loomed up behind Firespitter. It swept him back into the sea before he could get his lava blasts working again. Toby and the other children breathed a sigh of relief.

With Firespitter beaten, it took Mantra and Delos just minutes to capture Helico. They marched the defeated trio out of the water.

Razzle approached the Sea Gormiti and held out the amulet for Mantra to take. 'So, the legends were true,' she marvelled.

'There's only one way to find out,' smiled Toby.

'I have only one wish,' said Mantra. 'For my people to be free of Firespitter's spell.'

The amulet glowed brightly for a moment. Crabs and Helico shook their heads as they awoke from Firespitter's hypnotic trance.

Nervously, Firespitter began to tiptoe away, only for Crabs and Helico to grab him and pin him to the sand. He was going nowhere!

Mantra leaned down and handed Toby the amulet. 'You and your friends found the Lost Heart,' she said. 'The last two wishes are yours.'

'Sweet!' said Toby. 'I am *so* going to get an endless supply of ice cream for the rest of my life!'

'Toby!' snapped Jessica.

'I'm kidding! I wish this Keeper were back where he belongs – in the Primal Pad.'

A shimmering glow passed over Toby before he vanished, taking the amulet with him. The other children stood together with Razzle between them. They waved goodbye to Mantra and the Sea Gormiti as they were lifted through the portal to home.

Back in the pad, they found Toby lounging in the Keeper's chair.

'We've only got one wish left,' said Jessica.

'We'd better make it a good one,' added Lucas.

'Oh,' smirked Toby. 'I did.'

'You've already used it?' cried Nick. 'What did you wish for?'

'And lastly, I should be president of this club, because Nicholas Tripp is never, in a million years, going to find proof of the existence of an ancient civilisation, like a three-handled Hoachi pot.'

'Behold!' said a voice from the doorway.

Ike and the other club members looked over to see Nick smiling widely. In his hands he held an ancient-looking vase. *A three-handled Hoachi pot!'*

Ike's jaw dropped open and he let his list slip to the floor. All around him, the other club members leapt to their feet and raced over to Nick. Cheering, they hoisted him onto their shoulders and carried their club president along the corridor and out of the school.

Lucas, Jessica and Toby watched Nick be ferried

off to his victory celebration. 'You could have wished for anything. *Anything,*' Lucas groaned.

Toby smiled at the parade. He'd never seen his brother look so happy. 'Yeah, but ...' Toby nodded at Nick. 'What could be better than that?'

More stories and activity fun from the land of Gorm

Find another puzzle on the next page!

Odd One Out

One of these pictures of Nick is different from the rest. Can you spot the odd one out?

a   b   c   d

Answer: picture c is the odd one out. Nick's socks are different.

GORMITI
The Lords of Nature Return!

Primal Pad

Who will be today's Keeper –
Nick, Toby, Jessica or Lucas? Using a pencil cross out all
the letters that appear in the words PRIMAL PAD.

P	D	R	L	P	M	A	R	D	I
A	M	I	D	M	L	P	T	M	A
L	R	D	A	P	R	A	L	P	D
D	P	M	L	I	D	L	M	I	R
I	L	R	A	O	M	R	P	L	M
M	D	L	D	I	D	P	I	R	L
L	I	M	P	R	A	M	P	B	D
R	A	L	I	M	D	A	I	M	P
P	Y	R	A	R	I	L	R	A	I
D	I	M	D	P	A	R	D	L	P

Now write the remaining letters
below to reveal the Keeper: